Saints of Rush Lake

Saints of Rush Lake

Greg Klein

iUniverse, Inc.
New York Lincoln Shanghai

Saints of Rush Lake

iUniverse books may be ordered through booksellers or by contacting:

iUniverse
2021 Pine Lake Road, Suite 100
Lincoln, NE 68512
www.iuniverse.com
1-800-Authors (1-800-288-4677)

ISBN: 978-0-595-47346-5 (pbk)
ISBN: 978-0-595-91625-2 (ebk)

Printed in the United States of America

Dedicated to Aunt Rose.
She taught us to laugh and to treat each day as
if it was a special gift. She was a wonderful friend.

To Mom and Dad.
They were wonderful parents who provided a perfect
environment for us kids to grow up in.

ONE

Driving back from my childhood home of Atlanta, Michigan, on a crisp morning in late October, I thought that northern Michigan had never looked so beautiful. Just a few drab leaves still clung to the trees along the road, as if clinging to their last hope. Their recent dramatic palate of colors had changed to a dried brown shade and most had found their way to the ground. Those left still hanging were heavy with white frost, soon to fall. The evergreens were also white tipped, although they stood sturdy and tall against the elements, waiting to shrug off winter like a short nap in snow. It was like the earth was sucking up all the life into its insides to wait for the warming of spring. It was all beautiful, and it added to my feeling of happiness. I was smiling to myself and thinking about how wonderful it was to be alive. This had nothing to do with the recent visit with my family, although they do make me feel lucky to be part of their lives. One of life's necessities is to have people who care about you. Somehow, that connection of invisible roots to people that care for you keeps most people content to push through life, even though they're still looking for the greener grass.

No, this feeling had nothing to do with the weekend visit. This was about appreciating the wonders of being alive and a part of all of this beauty around me. It was like the kind of happiness when things in your life are in sync: my life, my family, and the relationship with my wife, Debbie. She was waiting for me in Indiana at the end of this trip. It was that kind of happy. The warmth of happiness inside pushed me into thinking of not only of people alive today, but of those from my past who have left this earth. I wished they were still here to enjoy all of this beauty around me. Maybe they were.

The hum of the tires and the strobing center lines coaxed me deep into thought. My mind started straying from happiness and the beauty around me to thoughts of the hereafter. Thinking of my grandparents always stirs those thoughts. Where are they? Are they watching? Are they happy? Is it wonderful up there, or is it nothingness? I will never be able to answer these questions, nor will anyone else. It's just our faith, or lack of it, that will help us to cope with the unknown.

One burning question from the weekend was still bothering me. One of my nieces, Jessica, asked my mom if she had any brothers or sisters. This took my mom by surprise, but more, it made me wonder how soon everyone forgets about

Mom, Rose and Glenn

those from the past, even those who were much too wonderful not to remember. Mom had a younger sister, Roselyn, who died years ago and an older brother, Glenn, who lives in Florida. He never comes around anymore because of a tragic circumstance with his son. Why didn't my niece know about these people? This was our fault, the older members of our family. It was our fault for not sharing the stories that made our family what it is today. These people are no longer with us, but they are still a part of the makeup of each and every one of us.

The mesmerizing road made me dream of these people. The scattered memories slowly pieced together in my head as if it was a script, as if it was their turn to take center stage to tell their story. I started to think of my childhood when things were simple and life was fresh and new. I soon forgot how long the journey back to Indiana was going to be as the cold thoughts of the hereafter slowly dissipated and wonderful times took over ...

It was a beautiful summer's morning and I was in the back seat of Aunt Rose's new '59 Chevy Impala, red and shiny with the convertible top down. Mickey, the terrier that went everywhere with Uncle Clifford and Aunt Rose, was in the back seat with me and my brother Mike. Mickey's tongue was slapping in the wind, spewing slobber around the car and all over Mike and me. When we hit Rush Lake Road, Aunt Rose told Clifford when to see how fast he could get this baby moving. She always liked to go fast and drink in all the fun and excitement of life. It was as if she knew her life on earth was going to be short. She had a childhood heart problem that could never be fixed and she lived a protected life, protected by all that loved her so she would be around to love for as long as possible.

We were on our way to Grandma Mowery's house. She and Grandpa ran a lakeside resort with cabins, boats, and a general store. It was the focal point of our summers at the lake, times that seemed magical, full of excitement and interesting characters from faraway places, come to join us at Rush Lake.

Summers were filled with fishing, exploring, and spending lazy days in the shade or sun. The breeze always filled the air with cool relief even on the hottest days. It was a child's dream.

When we arrived at Grandma's house, she came out to greet us by the tall hand pump in front of the grand summer home. This was the grand house where I spent many summers which seemed to be full of magic and excitement with characters that came from far away places to spend summers at Rush Lake. Grandpa and Grandma owned and operated the resort. They provided cabins, boats and ran a general store. They seemed to me to be the focal point of activities where many friends and customers came time and time again to enjoy their summer vacations. It was a child's dream to be part of it all.

Grandma was mad when she walked up to Clifford's car—we had made the thirty mile drive from Onaway in only twenty minutes.

"Rose Bug! You'll be the death of me someday!" she screamed Aunt Rose was too busy laughing, and as she walked by her mother, Rose reached out to tickle Grandma. "Stop that," Grandma said, but she began to laugh as loud as Rose. She forgave her in a moment's time.

I always felt like Aunt Rose was put on earth to make everyone laugh. Even Clifford, her husband, found her humor irresistible. He was big quiet man, kind of shy, but always smiling. He reminded me of a large kid that never grew up. He loved her deeply and they fit together like a hand in a glove. They were like two kids playing games through life, with no cares or worries. He had a hidden sense of humor that would burst out in the form of ingenious pranks that he played on all of us kids, mostly me. They couldn't have kids, but that didn't stop them from enjoying any of us kids that were close enough to prey upon. They always were our favorite aunt and uncle, and when the two of them were around, the pranks would start to flow. We would either be caught completely off guard or we would play straight man to add to the fun.

I was jolted back to the present when a deer suddenly appeared in the road ahead. Tingles rippled up my spine as I swerved quickly and the deer darted off into the woods. I slowed to see if any others were around. *Nothing. Whew, how close was that! I've got to stop daydreaming. I've got to start paying more attention,* I thought. A sign ahead said sixty-nine miles to Lansing. But within minutes, my mind started racing again as I thought about the past weekend and all the fun I had with my family. We are close. We get together most major holidays and always celebrate a reunion in the middle of each summer. It's a grand two-day event that takes a lot of energy to get through, but after it is over you are so glad you were part of it. You leave physically exhausted but spiritually nourished. We thoroughly enjoy each other's company, and after each get-together I feel I have filled up on enough laughter to keep me healthy until the next time we get together. We all are getting older, with my parents enjoying their final years in the warmth of Michigan summers and Florida winters. We are lucky to be so close. We do talk our gossip and we have our tiffs, but over all, we get along. None of us have ever had a major health problem, rare in a family of nine, all well into their adulthood. We are blessed. There I go. Blessed! That word. It makes me feel like I have just returned from a Sunday gospel sermon at the Atlanta Baptist Church with Reverend McPherson. Lucky is the word I would rather use. I don't believe that some higher force is responsible. It's luck that allows you to be part of a family like mine. To have us enjoy each other's company is even luckier. Luck is the word I would rather use.

I am the second eldest of the seven, with Mike the oldest. Mike and I were close enough in age that we shared most activities and friends. We played Little League baseball on the same team, went on camping trips with the Royal Rangers, and played Saturday afternoon baseball games with the neighborhood kids at the field down the street. We also spent many summers at the lake and a few times stayed with Aunt Rose at her house in the big city of Detroit. Because of all this, we share a hidden bond developed on the many playgrounds of childhood—forged with secrets of things we did that were kept from our parents. When we were older, we also shared late nights running the streets of downtown Atlanta.

My sister Amy is with Mike and me in the older group of kids. Our family is split into three groups, the older with Mike, Amy, and I, and the middle, a little younger group made up of Tammy, Tom, and Rick. Matt came along real late and is a group by himself. Amy was the little sister that we teased and protected at the same time. We played games with her when no one else was around to play. Sometimes we showed her gross things that we thought would make her sick, but we were surprised when she thought they were neat. Through it all, she looked up to us and that made us proud to be her older brothers. The three of us were the lucky ones since we remember all our grandparents and Aunt Rose. My feeling has always been that we are all built with blocks of memories from our past. The more people we have in our past to shape our future, the better person we become. The three of us benefited immensely from the long summers at the lake and lazy summer days growing up in a small town.

Knowing Aunt Rose meant knowing someone who loved life and loved to laugh. She always had tricks planned ahead, and she would spring them on Mike and me at just the right moment. Aunt Rose also played tricks on Amy. I remember one night at Grandma's house, Aunt Rose asked Amy if she had ever seen a falling star. "No," Amy said. So Aunt Rose gave her a rolled-up newspaper and told her to use it to look out into the night sky. Amy held it up to her eye. As she looked intently, peering for just a glimpse of a falling star, Aunt Rose slowly poured a glass of cold water down the other end. We all laughed. Even Amy. Tricks like these happened all the time when Aunt Rose was around. Once she got Mike good. She blackened a dish over the gas flame. When Mike came into the room, she gave him that dish, then took a clean one for herself. She told him to copy everything she did, and she ran her fingers around the bottom of the dish, then touched her face. Mike did the same. Soon Mike looked like an Indian with war paint on his face. We were all watching and trying not to laugh.

These memories are everywhere. Other memories have nothing to do with laughing, but with simple acts of kindness, like Grandpa cleaning and frying up the bluegill I caught one morning for lunch. He would join me and sit quietly and sing his unrecognizable tunes just under his breath. "Watch out for those bones!" he would say as he handed me a buttered piece of bread. These times are what I remember most.

"You think of Aunt Rose a lot, don't you, Greg?" said a voice. I had been deep in thought as a figure had formed next to me in the front seat of my car. I turned to find Grandpa Mowery setting next to me. He looked almost the same as I remembered him, except his breathing was noticeably easy, without the shallow, struggling breaths that he had to endure the last years of his life.

"What are you doing here, Grandpa?" I asked.

"I heard you talking," he said. "I thought you might need someone to talk to."

"Talk about what?" I asked.

"How everyone is doing," he said.

"Doing ... where?" I asked. He continued to talk in a kind of mono humming tone that blended in with the noise of tires on the road. He softly explained that everyone I think about is fine.

"They are thinking of you, too," he told me.

"They can see me?" I asked.

"Not like you would think. Not like you do in this world. It's more of a feeling," he explained.

Pressing down on the accelerator as I tried to think of my next question, I suddenly realized Grandpa wasn't there anymore. Had he been there at all? Was I dreaming? I could have been so deep in the memory that I dreamed his existence. *Yes, that was it. Ghosts don't appear to me. I don't believe in them. I still don't. This didn't happen.* Or so I told myself.

I remember helping Grandpa in the summers. He would have me bail boats and help Grandma clean cabins after people moved out. He operated the small general store so that people staying at the lake didn't have to drive all the way back to town to get supplies. Inside the store was a Coke ice chest that opened from the top. If I helped with some chores around the house, he would tell me I could go a pick out a pop. He also sold fishing supplies. The most important thing he sold was bait from the worm pit next to his garage. It was a buried cement cubical filled with rich, black dirt. He let me get worms for customers when he was busy. I loved doing chores for Grandpa. It always seemed to me that Grandpa couldn't get along without my help. I now realize that he made me feel that way ... important. That's something grandparents do for their grandkids. I realize that young men also do the same thing for their fathers and grandfathers who might feel a little underappreciated. My grandpa also did a lot of the cooking. He made great breakfasts. Mike's favorite was Famo pancakes, a brand of pancake mix long gone from grocery shelves. Mike always asked for them when he was there, but to me, Grandpa's tomatoes and eggs were the best. Whatever he cooked, we ate it and loved it.

Grandpa was a very quiet man but he seemed always to be singing or humming songs. The songs were not real songs, just tunes and melodies. He wore suspenders and gray pants ... every day. I never looked in his closet, but I imagined fifty pairs of the same gray pants hanging side by side. I never heard him raise his voice or say anything bad about anyone. He spent a lot of his time alone, but he had a few really close friends, like Max and Irene McCormick, for example, to socialize and drink a Drewrey's beer or two with him and Grandma.

Suddenly a voice interrupted the quiet.

"Charlie, your Grandpa was here, just like I am now." Charlie was the nickname my Grandma Mowery always called me. I hadn't heard it in years. I turned to find her sitting right next to me! I felt my face to see if I was conscious ... She was here!

"Please tell me you are really here, Grandma," I said.

"Yes, Charlie, I am real, and I am here. I wish you would believe in our world and not doubt yourself."

Silence hit me like never before. I was struggling for the next word—or was I waiting for her to explain why she was here? After seconds that seemed like minutes, I blurted out, "Grandma, can you tell me why you and Grandpa are here to talk to me?"

"You'll understand soon enough," she responded. "You were always too impatient, Charlie. Gullible and impatient. Don't you remember those times I took you fishing?" She laughed and added, "You wanted the fish to bite the minute your line went in the water. No patience. A good fisherman always has patience like your great-grandfather. Now he was a fisherman."

I asked her if she remembered the time she took me out fishing with a cane pole. She laughed and nodded. I caught a small pike and when I pulled it out of the water it swung back toward the boat and smacked Grandma on the side of her head. We both started laughing so hard the fish fell back in the water. I remembered her sitting in the middle seat with her head down and her whole body shaking and laughing until she had tears.

We rowed all the way back home from the far side of the lake, joking about the one that got away.

Silence struck again. Then I said, "I am sorry I wasn't with you when you died."

She smiled and replied reassuringly, "You were, Charlie. You won't understand yet, but we are all tied together through the brighter side. You were there …" and with that, she was gone.

I sat there, puzzled. How come this was happening? None of this made sense, yet it all made perfect sense. Why now? Why have they not come to me before in the dark of the night or down a lonely hallway? Why are they are here now? Would anyone believe me if I told them this happened?

I started thinking about how Tom would react. My brother Tom, a jokester, is the next in line of us kids. Tom is the kind of guy that fits in with any group of people at any age. He is a forty regular. He just fits. He has a wit about him that makes people want to be around him to laugh and forget their cares. At every family get-together there are always a few Tom stories that get told over and over so others can share in the laughs. If Tom heard about these people visiting me today, Tom would make a joke about it. He would probably say something like, "Greg, can I have some of that stuff you were smoking?" Or, "Yeah, Greg, *weeee* believe you," said while rolling his eyes at the rest of the family. That would be just like him. I started to rationalize the whole thing and soon began to laugh.

I knew the family would laugh, especially Tammy. She sometimes reminds me of Aunt Rose. She has the same sense of humor and even her mannerisms are so much like Rose's that you would say they were stitched from the same cloth. Tammy is my younger sister. Sadly, she didn't know Rose for very long. I always felt like they would have been inseparable, and for a short time, they were. They shared an affinity for children. Tammy had the enjoyment of having kids, and she is the kind of mom that I imagine Aunt Rose would have been. She is the kind of mom who took time to enjoy her kids. Roselyn would have been proud to see Tammy experiencing the humor and moments that evolve around a family while injecting her own style of clowning. Being loud and boisterous, Tammy is sometimes teased by the rest of the family about her charisma, but handles it with more of the same, only louder.

"Have you been out in my garden eating my raspberries?" a voice interrupted again.

Turning, I found a man in a gray hat sitting next to me. It really took me by surprise. It was Grandpa Klein. I had forgotten how he had looked. When people have been gone for years, their features become a blur in your memory, but here he was, as he had been in life. His face had deep wrinkles of strong character and dark skin from years of working outdoors. His eyes twinkled behind the glasses that I seemed to recollect from long ago. His smile made him very charming and endearing.

"I wished I had been eating them. They sure were good," I said.

He laughed.

Grandpa Klein

"I wish you were there, too. Maybe I could grow just one more garden with plenty for all?"

"Do you miss being there, Grandpa?"

"Missed is not the word. You don't miss anything here. You have everyone around you and you can feel everyone else in a way that is close and comforting," he explained.

"I do miss fishing and hunting, but those things are not as important in my world as they once were." I wondered what he meant by that, but

I didn't want to ask him. I struggled for things to talk to about. I realized he wouldn't be sitting here for long. He would soon disappear like the rest of them.

"Can we go fishing some time in your world, Grandpa?" I asked.

"Sure. It will happen."

I started to remind him a big fish story he told me about him and Uncle Phil. I really think the drink was to blame for this story.

"Remember the time you two went ice fishing on Valentine Lake in the winter and you caught that great big pike?"

He smiled and nodded.

"Its tail broke the side of the shanty when you pulled it out of the ice hole … at least that is the story, right, Grandpa?"

He started to laugh and then it slowly faded away as he left.

Why couldn't he stay and let me talk to him for a while? This whole thing was really starting to confuse me. People were popping in and out, but no one answered my questions and everyone was just telling stories to make me feel good.

A sign ahead read sixty-nine miles to Lansing.

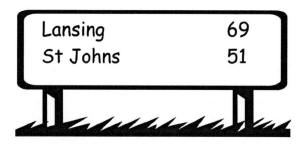

Two

Driving around the back roads on a lazy Sunday afternoon, Uncle Clifford spotted a pile of pop bottles under a tree about fifty feet off the road. The excitement in Aunt Rose's voice and the thought of all that free money just lying there waiting for me to pick up was too much.

"Stop the car!" I demanded.

Clifford quickly stopped and backed up to the spot. Aunt Rose told me to put them in the trunk. I got about halfway there when Clifford started slowly pulling away. I heard them both laughing as they did it. Scared to be left in the woods, I started running after them, forgetting the bottles and the money that could have been. Running with abandonment, I didn't notice that the car was bending back a branch until it released it with all the force of a batter swinging at a fastball. Smack! I ran right into it—or it ran into me. It knocked me down, but as it seems with every instance with Rose and Clifford, everything turned out all right. I was OK. We collected the bottles and all had a big laugh at my expense. These instances seemed to happen on cue when you were around the two of them.

One story started with a loose front baby tooth that was about to come out. Aunt Rose told me she knew a painless way to pull it. She tied a string around it and then tied the other end to the front door of Grandpa's store. She said when she opened the door from the inside, the string would tighten and pull the tooth out. She went inside, I stood outside. I held my head even with the knob so it would pull straight. Shaking in my boots, I waited for the door to open. Little did I know that the door opened toward me. Bam! The knob hit me smack in the mouth, knocking out the tooth, which was left dangling on the string tied to the doorknob. She was right, with all the pain of the knob hitting my mouth, I didn't notice the tooth pain at all. Aunt Rose swore she didn't know it opened that way, but as I grew older and reasoned it out, the story seemed too far-fetched to believe. It's a wonder I survived all of her antics.

My mom and Aunt Rose were not only sisters, but also best friends. They shared everything, secrets, laughs, and a big brother named Glenn. Mom and Glenn were very popular kids in school. Roselyn wasn't quite on the same level but only because of her delicate condition. Like my grandpa and grandma, Rose's siblings protected her with love. Mom was not only popular, but very beautiful. That's how she grabbed the fancy of my dad, even though he was much older. She won the local beauty contest at the 4H Fair when she was seventeen. Dad was well liked by most in town. He was the catcher on the town's baseball team, and a very good ball player at that. Under the right circumstances, he could have made baseball his profession. He had other plans. He also fell in love. With looks that rivals envied and the charms of boyish grins, he made her his own. He was destined to become her forever man. Marilyn and Vernon are together today. They are living between the sunshine of Florida and the sunshine of Lake Fifteen in Atlanta, with the family constantly chasing them in droves wherever they settle for a short period. Sometimes I feel they are running from us. Dad doesn't seem to mind as long as he has a place to have a few drinks, a stirring conversation, and a quiet nap in the afternoon. He has become a pilot in his later years and has taken to the skies to find his peace. He shares his new world with anyone who wants to enjoy the view from God's steps. Flying has become a passion with him, and his chariots are the planes he rebuilds. He finds abandoned old relics and restores them to the promise for which they were built years before. Repapered and brightly painted, they fly together as if both have been restored.

He is riding his bike to the ball field …

The leaves have fallen off the trees of your seasons
and the frost is showing in your hair,
I've watched you from afar admiring your family with
a pleasant and thoughtful stare.
These times show me insight into this man who's my father,
without voicing even a cry.
He touts his pride of his life with a smile and his deep love
with a twinkle in his eye.

I've watched him across the fire at night as his face
has shown the reflection of his father.
He's an old man now, not the youngster from past,
but still lives his days without bother.
It is said you take only your character with you to the life
that is beyond all that exists.
He will need a large trunk, I've often surmised,
for he has too much to carry in his fists.

He is riding his bike to the ball field … again …

Dad

"Do you understand now why I preached so hard for you to get good grades?" A voice and figure suddenly appeared at my side as if to join in on my conversation with myself. It was Grandma Klein. She was the epitome of what a school teacher should look like. She had a very stern face, with just enough love showing through her eyes to make even the most scared child in trouble stand and take his punishment. She spoke with perfect grammar and expected you to do the same.

"I wasn't handing out dollars for As on your report cards without a purpose," she said.

"Yes, I do understand now Grandma," I replied, as if answering the teacher's question in class.

She continued to explain, "You get out of life just what you put into it, and if you cheat along the way, you only cheated yourself." She wasn't scolding me, just stating facts. "I know you didn't cheat yourself, Greg, I was watching," she said.

"Watching?" I asked. "How long have you been watching?"

She looked at me and her face turned to a kindness like I have never seen from her before as she said, "All your life." With that, she smiled and was gone. The smile seemed to linger in the air for some time after I realized the seat was empty. Somehow I knew she would be back. I was beginning to become rather accustomed to these comings and goings. In fact, I was starting to really enjoy them. But still, I wondered. All of my life? What did she mean? *It's not over yet,* I thought. What a strange statement.

This was becoming a strange trip home. I started to think about getting home and how much I missed being there. Besides Debbie, my dogs will be there to greet me as soon as I walk in. Sophia will run and jump up on me and Yancy, my basset, will come running down the hall with his tail wagging frenziedly. I've often wondered, if there is a heaven, do dogs go? If they do go to heaven, who judges which ones make it into heaven? If dogs go to heaven, what about everything else? Cats? Horses? Wild animals? What would the cutoff be? Ants? Worms?

Didn't God create all of these? At least that is what religious people say. Grandma Klein once told me the Bible says, "Even the lowly blade of grass." Do I believe it? Buddhist, Catholics, Presbyterians, Muslims … they all have their own version. If dogs do go to heaven, who do they see when they get there? Their masters? Their family? Only other dogs? We were their masters and what they lived for and all they knew on earth, so wouldn't they want to be with us when we arrive? The thought of not ever seeing the pets of my past gave me an empty feeling inside. All these unknowns without answers made me feel uncomfortable. I quickly returned to the weekend of fun with my family where I seemed to have some answers and control.

We have a tendency to drink a little too much when we get together. This invariably adds to the number of laughs and lengthens the evenings to well beyond normal hours. Nobody seems to miss the sleep. It's the fun you really don't want to miss out on. Mostly it's just our family, but we have some close friends that are considered part of the family. One couple that comes to mind is Mary and Joe Cauchon. Joe was my dad's best friend growing up. He and Mary lived in the same area in northern Michigan until soon after their marriage. With a family started and a need to provide, Joe moved to the big city and found work with the auto industry. Although they moved away, they stayed close to our family. They continued to vacation up north and spend time with us every chance they got. Their two sons were close in age to Mike and me, and the twins were Amy's age. Our families vacationed together many times, and we also traveled to Detroit to stay with them once or twice.

Joe was a funny man. Yes, was. Sadly, he is no longer with us. He died a few years ago. Mary stays in the same park in Florida where Mom and Dad live and where she and Joe spent lots of winters enjoying the warmth of the sun and their many friends. She is moderately coping with life after Joe. Living with all the residual love and happiness he brought her for years, she continues to be an inspiration to those who live without essential parts of life.

Joe was essential. He loved Mary very much. He loved his family. He loved life. Although there were tragedies—he lost his oldest son to mental illness and one of the twins to suicide—he continued to keep his sense of humor and zest for life. Joe spent his life unselfishly working and living where he didn't want to be, all for the love of providing for his family. When retirement finally came, he quickly moved north where he and Mary became a close part of our family again by physically planting roots, in the form of a trailer, right on my parent's property while he had a cabin built. With an extension cord to our house, a kind of an umbilical cord to our family, he had all the comforts he and Mary needed. This made it easy for them to quickly become friends with many of the people that surrounded my parent's social life. He would also play his guitar for our family get-togethers and summertime campfires.

He and Mary would spend the days in a casual manner, going shopping, visiting friends, reading, doing crossword puzzles, and of course, drinking a few highballs in the afternoons of the summer heat. When the cabin was finished, it quickly became a hot spot for people to come and go and to enjoy. He called it his Lily Pond Shack. Joe grew no grass. Too much work. Sand was the landscape of choice. It fit nicely with the trail to the riverfront. In fact, a prickly pear started to grow one spring in the front yard. It quickly became as big as small tree. Joe decorated it as a Christmas tree. Once, while Joe and Mary were in Florida, their friends made fun of them by videotaping a party they held at their cabin. They sent them a copy of the tape. I'm sure Joe thought it was hilarious.

Dad and Joe

I miss Joe. He called me his biggest fan, as if he was always on stage. The minute he would see me he would start in with a routine that was worthy of Youngman or Dangerfield, and I would start laughing till tears filled my eyes. Joe and Mary went to Florida one year and he quickly took ill. I thought I would eventually hear good news that he was recovering and would soon be released from the hospital. It didn't happen.

When I learned of Joe's passing, I remembered thinking for the second time in my life, why would God take anyone like this human from earth? What would be the purpose to leaving one of them alone? This helped support my feelings of life as a random existence. No rules. No ruler. No god. Even so, I rationalized God's existence by thinking that God was selfish and wanted to laugh like the people that hung out with Joe. He wanted him to play guitar and tell jokes by his campfires.

As I drove on, an accustomed feeling came over me. I wasn't sure why, but everything started to seem like I had been there before. Sort of like déjà vu, not a feeling, but being there and seeing things recently, over and over again.

Without dwelling on it, I started thinking back to my childhood again and the people that were special to me. My family lived on a lake most of our lives. While we grew up in a small ranch house my dad built near the small town of Atlanta, we spent most of the summers at Rush Lake.

When I was in my teens, we moved to a house my dad had built on Crooked Lake. That was the last house I lived in with my family. I left for college and then the Air Force and started my family somewhere in between. My folks moved to their current house, which my dad built on Lake Fifteen a few years after I had moved on. This house is where we started the tradition of the summer reunions. Originally attended by immediate family and only a few close friends, it was an all-day nonstop whirl of games, food, and a campfire after dark. The guitar playing, stories, and nonstop jokes lasted until the early morning.

The later ones consisted of family, friends of family, friends of friends, friends of someone who thought they were a friend, and anyone within twenty miles and looking for a fun time or a free beer. To give some idea of how they developed, Matt, the youngest, was a tiny toddler at our first one. He would start crying when he was trying to hit a ball with a plastic bat but couldn't. Today he is one of the largest in size, a superb mixologist of drinks, a big drinker, a walking song and artist encyclopedia—but he still cries because he can't swing a bat and hit a ball. Some things don't change.

My Family

Matt doesn't remember Aunt Rose or any of his grandparents except Grandpa Mowery. Grandpa spent his last days in a home for the elderly in Alpena. On reunion weekends, someone would make the hour and half trip to get him. He would sit with all of us for a few hours in the early afternoon until his breathing tired him. Then someone took him back to the home. Did he want to stay? I often thought about how he felt and what he was thinking.

"Yes, I wanted to stay," he said answering my thoughts from the passenger seat of my car. "What do you think?" He appeared in mid-thought as if he were listening all along to my conversation with myself. "Even though I wasn't talking much or being part of the conversations around me, I was enjoying it. I loved being there. I did have that misery of nicotine constantly distracting me and my breathing made me exhausted quickly, but I was enjoying it. I wish I could have stayed longer," he lamented. "I enjoyed watching all you kids. I wished Mary could have been there to see everybody and how everyone turned out. Little did I know at the time she was with us."

He continued, "You see, Greg, we are all here to enjoy each other's company, and that continues after death ... Life is just a beginning."

With that he left. Question answered.

My thoughts were spinning out of control. I started to focus again on the long drive home. It seemed to be much longer this time around. Why were all these spirits coming in and out of my car? I wanted this trip to end. I wasn't hungry nor did I feel the need to stop and stretch, and the sights and sounds of my surroundings were in a distant fog. Maybe I wasn't concentrating enough on my driving.

I had to get back to pleasant thoughts like those I was enjoying when I started this drive.

THREE

Aunt Rose was getting dressed at my grandma's lake house one morning. She was almost dressed when she saw a car going down the road about a hundred yards away. She shouted to my little sister Tammy, "Oh my gosh, someone might have seen me! Tammy, run down the road and see if you can see my boobies."

Tammy being very young, unsuspecting, and easy prey, did just that. She ran down the road and looked back to see if it was possible. When she got to the spot where Rose told her to run, she looked back to see if she could see Aunt Rose in the window. She could hardly see the window, let alone her boobies. She instantly knew she had been taken; even though she was a little girl, she could figure that out. She started to laugh. Another victim, another laugh.

Mike and I used to spend a few weeks during the summer with Aunt Rose in the city. This was even more of a vacation than Rush Lake because we could stay up all hours of the night watching multiple channels on TV. We only had three stations up north and they went off the air at 11:30 in the evening. We would order Little Caesar's pizza and have it delivered right to our door at night! Can you believe it? Scary movies, cartoons till all hours and pizza to our door! What more could a kid ask for? Uncle Clifford worked long hours and was gone very early in the morning, but when he got home, the fun would start. One evening after dinner we were sitting around the small living room when Uncle Clifford popped out of the kitchen with a can of whipped cream for the strawberry shortcake that Aunt Rose was busy fixing. He showed us that if you hold out your tongue and just barely hit the nozzle, you would get a golf ball-sized sweet surprise. He did it to himself, and then he demonstrated it on Mike. No problem. So I gave the go-ahead. I held my tongue out and he stood there for a minute, which added to the excitement, then bam! He held the nozzle down until within a second my mouth was full and whipped cream was overflowing all over my face. He just kept spraying until I was covered.

Aunt Rose was coming into the living room with dishes of strawberries. She started to laugh so uncontrollably that she dropped to her knees and flung the strawberries. Plates hit Mike sitting on the couch. Strawberries were everywhere, I was covered in whipped cream, and as if that wasn't enough, Clifford turned and sprayed cream on to Aunt Rose's head as if to make a hat. Mickey was busy licking up the whipped cream from the floor and eating the dropped shortcake. After the food fight we still had some of the shortcake left to eat. We cleaned up later with laughs and giggles.

To me, their life seemed full of such laughs and giggles. I am sure they had their times of worrying and anger, but I didn't see them. I never remember Clifford or Rose being mad at each other. I never saw them argue. They were always fun and lighthearted. Money was never mentioned. I am sure they didn't have much, but they didn't seem to need it. I felt the warmth of her laughter fill me inside, and suddenly that warmth took me to another time and place …

I was lying on a dock on a hot summer's day, peeking through a crack to watch my bait dangle in front of a large rock bass hiding in the shade of the dock. The sun was slowly turning my back beet red. I didn't notice because a boy with a cane pole and a can of worms on Rush Lake in the summer was in Paradise. Suddenly a fish moved forward and the bait disappeared. I tugged and found it securely hooked. As I pulled the line up, I realized I hadn't really thought this one out. The line was through the middle of the dock and the fish was too big to pull through the crack in the boards. What was I to do? Grandpa just happened to be walking down the road in front of the lake, coming back from a visit to one of his friends. He quickly saw my predicament and started to laugh. He came over to hold the line and told me to get in the water. I did, reaching under the dock to retrieve the fish. We walked home together, me with my unusual catch. I never saw Grandpa go fishing, so I asked if he liked to fish. He said he did but he didn't have time. He explained that he always had too much to do around the lake and the house helping Grandma. I felt like he was there to make others happy to be at his lake for the summer. I thought if I helped him real hard he would have time to go. He never did.

The road took us up the hill to the corner where you could get a view of Little Lake. To a child with a vivid imagination, this was a mysterious lake. It was dark and deep, with a very mucky bottom. The only one place to get to its shoreline was a trail that went down though the swamp that surrounded the lake. The trail broke out to a small clearing where an old boat was tied to the shore. Grandpa had told us the story of his horse getting caught in its mucky bottom. It was sucked under and drowned. One year, Mike and I found a skull in the muck near the shore. We were certain it was the horse's head. Looking back, I realize it was probably a deer or some small animal, but to us it was the horse's head, and that added to the enigma of the lake.

Years later I was fishing on the lake with my little brother Rick when we spotted an unrecognizable creature swimming near the shore. It was long, with a few humps out of the water trailing behind as if it was snakelike. It would disappear and reappear at random. We chased it for a while but could not get close enough to see what it was. To this day I still get chills thinking about what we saw that day.

Grandpa and Grandma always warned Mike and me about being around Little Lake because of the unknown danger. We used that fear to bring creatures and ghosts stirring within our young minds. The mystery of that lake still haunts me.

As I drove, I started to visualize some of the faces that were part of the Rush Lake of my early years. My great-grandpa was one that came to mind. I remember him as a large, funny old man that always seemed to be wearing red suspenders. He was always barefooted, with his pants rolled up. He had a head of white hair that was never combed. His whiskers were also white, with a mustache that he would tickle us with when he wanted us to laugh. He was always smiling. Sometimes he would wear a black patch over his missing eye, and that made him look like a character from *Huckleberry Finn*. Most of all, he was a true outdoorsman. He found time for fishing and hunting. He always fished alone and never told where he went to catch those big, dark beauties from the lake. "Secret spots," he would say. He would come back with large pails of bluegill or stringers full of huge bass and pike that he would dump at our feet on the boards by the tall pump in front of the house. He would laugh like Santa at the enjoyment of watching Mike and me in our excitement as we held up the fish to imagine what it would have been like if we had been there with him.

He loved his lake. He loved his tobacco and he loved his beer. I remember he used to have a black bear as a pet. He brought it out to show people how it would drink beer from a bottle. He also had an old hound that would chase us kids if we ran. The old dog would scare us to death when he chased us as if he was going to eat us. Sometimes you would forget about the dog being around and start running. The howling would start and you knew the dog had spotted you and was running after you. This made you think … run faster or stop? I never did stop—never had the courage.

I don't remember much about my great-grandma. My memories consist of her always in bed, or sometimes on the porch where she could watch outside and get some warmth from the sunshine. She had to be fed by Grandma or Great-Grandpa, who took turns. I remember wondering when she was going to get better and start walking around like the rest of us. She never did, of course. In fact, I don't remember when she died. When it happened, the kids were probably told that she went away for a while. That was the common way to help explain the situation without getting a lot of questions back.

Great-Grandpa's was the first death I can remember being told about. I was too young to understand, but remembering back, I realize that I thought I would never see Rush Lake again. I thought everything was going to change in my life. In a strange way, I was right. It was never the same again. One large part of it was gone for good. As a child, I didn't really notice, but as I grew, I missed his presence. The only change I noticed at the time was that Grandma and Grandpa moved from their little house into the big two-story white house.

Our family, once or twice, spent a week in the summer there using the little house as a vacation home, and sometimes Grandma used the kitchen to help prepare Thanksgiving dinners. When Mike and I had friends stay with us at the lake, we slept in that house, which was attached to the big house. We were all by ourselves, and I remember staying up late and telling scary stories—not a good idea when sleeping in an old house by yourselves. Thunderstorms and creaky floors would heighten the suspense, sometimes to the point where we would grab blankets and go next door to sleep on the floor downstairs. The scariest night, though, was the night Mike and I were sleeping on the bed in the living room alone in the house. In the middle of the night, Paul Harman came pounding on the picture window and screaming at the top of his lungs for help. When Mike and I awoke to the terrifying screams, we saw Old Man Harman in the window, while in the background was his house on the hill in full blaze. We watched the rest of the night in horror as the house burnt to the ground.

During the hunting season my grandma and grandpa took in hunters from out of town for a little extra money. Eventually it turned into a seasonal thing where the store was turned temporarily into a bunk house. They had between twenty and twenty-five men from all over the area for at least the first week every deer season. The numbers dwindled after that. Mike and I stayed at the lake as much as possible during that time. We got up at 3:30 to help them get breakfast ready at 4:30 in the morning and helped pack separate lunches for the hunters from the leftovers of the meal the night before. Then we helped clean the bunk house while the guests were out hunting. Soon it was time for dinner. Grandma put on a huge feast each evening. I loved to sit and hear the guys tell stories about their daily hunt. After the dishes were done I could go and join them while they drank, told stories, and played

Greg in the Hunters Camp

cards. A few hunters would stay as long as Thanksgiving, when they would join our family for our meal, but most had either killed their deer by then, or had had enough of being away from their family and work and gone home. The ones that stayed were close friends and really didn't have anything to go home to.

"Dangerfield?" a voice asked. "I rival Rodney?"

I knew in an instant it was Joe Cauchon.

"No, Sydney Dangerfield," I replied, trying to be funny. "Underwear salesman from Cleveland."

He laughed, which made me laugh and I knew that grin would be hard to remove from my face for a while. It's one of those grins that hurts after a while. "What are you doing here?" I asked.

"Thought I would stop in and welcome one of my biggest fans," he said.

"Welcome?" I replied. No response. After a minute of silence I noted, "Sorry I didn't make your funeral or tribute. Work was too much at the time. Damn AT&T. I wrote a great eulogy that I was going to give. It was funny and touching. I was proud of myself."

"I heard it," he said. "It was good—considering the source."

I chuckled and grinned harder.

"It was good ... but your dad's was better. You got married again after I left, huh?" he asked.

"Yes. Wish you could have met her. She would be your number two fan," I said. "She laughs like I do, all the time, only louder." Trying to keep him from leaving too quickly I tried to think of a question to ask him. "Do you know how Mary is doing?"

"Yes," he said. "She is fine and well looked after. I watch her at night while she sleeps. She doesn't need much care because she has John and Judy and many wonderful friends. She also knows I'm there with her. The one I watch the most is Joey."

The silence came with the word Joey. Silence and sadness inside. Joey was his oldest son who was taken from him by mental illness years before. It's like he disappeared into another world.

"I always will envy your life, Joe. You had so much fun."

"Never envy someone else's life. You don't know what happened when the lights went out. Whether you're rich, poor, happy, or sad, the grass always looks greener on the other side of the hill. Be happy with yourself."

With that Joe was gone, but the grin was still there. It started to hurt my face because it had been there for so long—a good hurt. I started to think about the trip back home and how it seemed to be taking so much longer this time.

Joe Couchon

FOUR

One summer's morning, Uncle Clifford woke Mike and me very early
to tell us the exciting news that he was going to take us fishing. Now,
normally that would be enough to make
us jump out of bed at 6 a.m. without a
second thought, but we knew the day
before Uncle Clifford had gone fishing
with Bill Kelly from down the lake. He
had showed Clifford his secret spot to
get the biggest bluegills on the lake. So
with even more anticipation, we jumped out of bed to quickly dress.
Grandpa was already up to see us off and to make us breakfast. While
we were eating, he went out on the porch off the kitchen and picked
out just the right cane poles. He always stored them on the roof of the
little house. Only adults could reach them. Next, he and I went to the
worm pit to get a big can of fat juicy ones. Now we were ready. Down
the lake we went to row out to the spot which Clifford had carefully
marked with landmarks from the shore. "I think it was about two hundred yards out from that A-frame," he said as he pointed to shore. Soon
we were over the deep black area with just the faint sight off weeds
coming up from the deep. "This is it," Clifford yelled. "Drop the anchor."
With that, we started the most productive couple of hours of bluegill
fishing that I could have imagined. Big dark beauties took bobber after
bobber down to the depths until we were tired of pulling them up and
baiting our hooks.

We joked and teased each other on whose fish was the biggest or the smallest. Soon the sun was high in the sky and bearing down on us, and the fishing activity slowed. The short night of sleep started creeping into my eyes, making everything look a little cloudy. The waves had died down to an almost glassy calm. The fun and laughs slowed to a pensive mood. The fishing was done. We loaded the large stringer of fish into the boat and lifted anchor. On the way back, I quietly reflected about Great-Grandpa, wondering if this was one of the secret spots he had fished so many times. If it was or wasn't I would never know, but I know he was proud watching us use his lake to have the time of our lives. I'm sure he was smiling from above.

Rush Lake had a magical hold on the people that were tied to its unending waves and sandy shores. While the birth of my mom and dad's first child should have been the biggest event of their abbreviated love, it turned out to be a circumstance to shake your soul to the core. David died soon after birth. These life experiences seem to bring a young man's conscience and emotions to the surface. Dad picked up his son from the hospital and with the little casket in the front seat of his car, drove him around the roads that surround the lake, speaking to him softly of the wonders he would see in his life as if he was soon to be part of it all. The words will never be spoken again, but I am sure David was listening intently to every sound, every word from Dad's mouth.

Grandpa had ten cabins to care for and rent out during the long summers. He sold three of them one year, but even seven cabins and a dozen boats kept him hopping all summer long. Three cabins were located up on the hill next to the big white house while the other four were on the lake. Number Ten, the big one, was one of the cabins on the lake, and Grandpa let Mom and Dad use it for a week in July every year. This was a cheap vacation for our family even though my dad continued to work. These weeks were special. The days weren't long enough. We ran from daylight until well into the night. A few times we had friends stay next to us. Sometimes our close friends the McElroys stayed on one side in their grandpa's cabin and the Browns were on the other side in one of Grandpa's cabins. Each family had plenty of kids that were close in age. This made for even longer days and nights.

The days were filled with boating, fishing, and exploring. The nights were bonfires and ghost stories, chase games, and night swimming. Parents usually gathered to mix drinks and play cards well into the night. That made it easier for us to play on the large lawn in front of Harman's cabins, usually until late in the cooling night when the dew started to gather and the stars seemed to be so large and bright you could jump and reach them. This is when we usually had bonfires and told ghost stories.

Some of my early childhood crushes were sparked with young girls from faraway places who were vacationing at the lake. Some barely knew my name and the rest I only knew as passing friends and a face across a fire that mesmerized a young heart for a few days during the summer. Those nights and faces are a distant memory now, but they will remain a part of me forever. Sometimes while I'm talking with friends about my childhood, I describe how fun-filled mine summers were, and most of that fun revolved around our adventures at Rush Lake.

Those were the best of times. What I wouldn't give to relive one of those weeks. The cabin we stayed in was even more special. Wood floors and walls that didn't run to the ceiling meant every noise in every room was heard all night long. I remember one night listening to a static-filled radio broadcast of my beloved Tigers and Red Sox battling it out. Kaline, my hero, tied it late in the game, but Jim Rice hit a ninth-inning home run to win it for the Red Sox. Mom kept telling me to turn it down.

Noise was everywhere, but we didn't mind. Water in the kitchen was from a small pump. Screen doors that creaked loudly when opened and slammed shut on the spring helped with the essence of rustic living. An outhouse for the necessities added to the overall appeal. Baths were a dip in the lake first thing in the morning, sometimes with soap and shampoo. We all helped with the dishes and most chores in the morning, but the laundry was done by Mom up at Grandma's house in the old wringer washer.

After the chores, it was off to the lake to fish or swim. If we caught fish we had to clean them in the swamp behind the cabins. There was a trail to get to an old table in a small clearing. Mosquitoes were bad and rabid for young blood. Both hands were busy and very messy so the critters had an open invitation to bite at will. You cleaned as quickly as you could and buried the waste in the pit nearby. If you were lucky and the fish was big enough, you nailed the head to the tree for all to see. Some had been there for years. I envisioned that a few were caught by my great-grandpa, even though, deep down, I really didn't think so because I knew he wouldn't brag about his fish. He was a real sportsman.

As I drove, I noticed the surroundings were becoming more bland, almost like elevator music—just background noise. I was not hungry, so the normal stop at the new outdoor mall in East Lansing wouldn't be necessary. It seemed like it was still miles away. Even after all this time and all these conversations, I was hardly moving.

I started to think of Debbie, missing her smile. She had come along at a very lonely time of my life. She made me consider my future and all the wonderful things to enjoy in this world. She appreciates the same things that I do and shares in my enjoyment. Not until I met Debbie, I never before understood that kind of love. Now when I see other couples in the same kind of relationship, I feel their hidden uncertainty of the future and the pain they hide within. I hope they have the chance someday to meet someone who makes them feel warm life deep inside. That's how I feel. That's Debbie. She loves me unconditionally. She loves my passions. She loves to travel to far-off places. She loves good food and she loves wine. Wine is one of my passions and she has grown to love it with almost the same intensity as me. Almost, but not quite. She also loves to fish. I thought last summer was the perfect time for me to share Rush Lake with Debbie. The draw to share its persona with loved ones is inevitable. I had wanted to make the journey back myself many times in the past, but the apprehension of it not living up to my memories made me weary of the journey. We went anyway.

We rented a cabin from friends of ours and brought our dogs along for fun. Debbie fell in love with the lake and was hardly ever out of the boat. The dogs followed in her passion. Sophia, our spaniel, carefully hawked the bobber's movements and excitedly watched each hooked fish back to the boat. Yancy, the bassett, didn't pay much attention to anything until a frenzied fish was flopping around the bottom of the boat. Minutes later, snuggled in his orange doggie life preserver, he would doze off in the warm sunshine and the rocking of the boat. Debbie fished from the dock when we were too tired to go out and she impatiently prodded me to get started early each morning.

One morning, it was too windy to fish so we decided to walk the back roads of my childhood. As we walked with the dogs, I visually painted the portraits of the people that lived in the cabins along the shore and pointed out the exact places where stories of my youth took place. As the day went on I continued to share my past. I slowly realized that my trepidations of coming back to this wonderful lake were unfounded, as everything was there except the faces of the people from long ago. I realized that on that remarkable day I had unveiled to Debbie the saints of Rush Lake.

Fɔvє

I was getting too tired to drive. I leaned back and rested my head on the back of the seat. My eyes slowly shut—just for a bit, it seemed. It felt good. The warmth of the sun … the warmth? I was in my car! Quickly opening my eyes, I saw nothing but deep blue sky above me. The gentle lapping of waves against the dock posts made a comforting rhythmic sound. I lifted my head enough to see Goldie, my grandma's cocker spaniel walking down the sunny road next to the lake toward the old maid's house. She spent most of her time there, and late in her life she even ended up living with them, which was no surprise to anyone. Grandma didn't mind.

Bill Kelly was in his yard across the street. He yelled to me something about how the fish were biting. "I'm not going fishing today," I answered. *I am not fishing today?* I thought to my self. *So, if I am not going fishing, what am I going to do today? I could run to the backwaters and catch frogs and turtles at the pond. I could throw bottles and rocks down the quarry by the trailer on the hill. I could go get Mike and play catch in Grandpa's field.*

I ran back to Grandma's to see if Mike was up and ready. When I got there he was just finishing getting dressed. I asked him if he wanted to play ball. He told me that Grandma and Aunt Rose had gone to Canada Creek to get groceries and pick up Guy Lowe, Mike's friend from school. "We're alone for now. Let's get out the magazines!" he said. Grandma had a huge collection of *True Romance* and *Real Detective* magazines.

They were stacked inside the hidden doors in the walls of the living room. We would throw a bunch on the floor in front of the large black heater, which was quiet now, in the summer, but in the winter it would bang and clang like it was alive. The noises would scare you when you were watching something like the *Untouchables* late in the evening. The magazines always had a sexy girl on the cover and had short stories with terrified woman or dark figures at the beginning of each story. The women were wearing something that would make a young man's imagination run wild, like a half-torn dress or nightgown that didn't cover much. The stories were scary and seductive at the same time. Usually some girl was being chased by a stranger, and I couldn't tell if she did or didn't want to get caught. We perused the pages for a while but soon we started to worry that Aunt Rose and Grandma would get home early, so we quickly stacked the magazines back in the cabinet and moved the chair back.

I asked Mike if he wanted to play catch. I knew his answer even before the words got out. He didn't like baseball as much as I did, and sure enough, he said he didn't. Guy was coming, and he was going to stay overnight. He said he was going to hang out with him. Guy was a cool kid but he would rather do cool grown-up things instead of fun boy stuff. He liked girls and cigarettes, not fishing and catching frogs. So I knew I was on my own that day.

Grandma and Aunt Rose finished putting away the groceries while Mike and Guy had left to go check out some girls. Guy seemed to always know where girls were staying at the lake or on the ranch. Grandma and Grandpa were going to visit Max and Irene and their crazy wiener dog. I had spent an embarrassing evening at their cabin once when the dog wouldn't stop humping my leg. They all thought it was funny and laughed the whole time. It seemed like hours. I didn't want to ever see that dog again. Aunt Rose could tell I was down, so she asked me if I would like to look at some of Grandma's magazines. I think she already knew Mike and I had scrutinized every page that morning. She would secretly let us look at them from time to time, making fun of the big boobies that some of the girls had in the pictures. She would call them my girlfriends and tease me. I told her I didn't want to look at the magazines so she asked if I wanted to go for a walk. Sounded like fun, even though I knew she couldn't walk very far. "Where are we going?" I asked. She didn't respond with a direct answer, so I became uneasy, thinking she was going to lead me off to another prank. We started off toward the big hill with the big sign made up of all the little white signs showing people who lived on the lake. It faced the dead end of the road that led to the lake. We stopped to read some of the names and to make fun of the funny sounding ones.

"Pepper ... Pickled Pepper," she blurted out, and we laughed.

"Croft ... Croft Cheese," I shouted and again we laughed. This went on for a while and then I threw a few stones at some trees and signs that Aunt Rose picked out for me to hit. As we walked back toward the house we stopped at the old tire swing tied to the tree by the side of the little house. She pushed me for a while and then when her breath seemed to be leaving her, I told her it was time to go back to the house.

I realized we hadn't walked more than a couple hundred feet in total, but all she wanted to do was cheer me up and spend some time with me before lunch. She was a kid at heart, and she probably had just as much fun with the walk as I did.

When we finished, we found Mike and Guy on the porch at the big house. Grandma had made us sandwiches and served them out on the porch. We ate lunch while Mike and Guy told us the girls had left to go to town for a while and would be back later. The boys were going back to their cabin after lunch. Grandma asked if I wanted to go to town to the biegarten later today. That's what she called the bar. I think it was from their German heritage. They were going to town for staples and some medicine from the drug store. I told her that I would love to go.

After lunch, Mike and Guy asked me to go with them to old horse barn. Little did I know that Mike had taken a pack of cigarettes from Grandpa's hutch. When the three of us got to the barn, they told me what they had done. Mike and Guy lit up one while they made me watch for anyone coming. It didn't take long for Grandpa to find out.

I don't know how, but he acted as if someone had told him. Grandma was furious. She told Guy he had to call his parents and go home. Mike and I were in trouble for a while, but Grandma knew it was the influence from elsewhere that made us do it, and she quickly forgave us. We knew we had done wrong and we were thankful we were forgiven, even though they were going to tell Mom and Dad.

Guy didn't look so cool when his parents arrived. Bob and Elsie Lowe owned the bar at Canada Creek Ranch. It was a long drive for them and it was in the middle of the business day while the bar was still open. This only made the situation worse for Guy. They apologized and took him away. He was crying when I saw him getting into the car.

After they left, Grandma said it was time to go to town. Grandpa drove while Aunt Rose sat in the backseat with us kids. When we got to downtown Atlanta and parked in front of the drug store, Grandpa and Grandma went in to get their medicine. Aunt Rose took me and Mike to the fountain in the back to have a coke. We told Grandma and Grandpa we would meet them later at the bar. They got their medicine and left.

Aunt Rose ordered me a Coke with chocolate syrup in it. She had ice cream in a glass with Coke poured over it. She let me taste it. Wow, it was good. I had had that once with root beer, but not Coke. We left for the bar after we drank our Cokes. When we passed the sport shop, Aunt Rose said we needed to go inside to look around. I liked to shop there where there was lots of neat fishing stuff. Aunt Rose bought me a couple of bobbers and a package of hooks. Mike got a small pocket knife.

When we got to the bar we found Grandpa and Grandma sitting at a table with their Drewreys half empty in front of them. Mike and I ordered Cokes that came in small glasses, each with a tiny straw. It didn't look like you could suck much Coke through it, but I tried anyway. Just the sight of me sucking desperately on a stirring stick made everyone laugh.

We jumped back into the car and headed home, admiring the treasures we had in our hands. We thanked Aunt Rose again.

I was so excited to get back to the lake. Somehow it always draws me back, the thrill of your bobber disappearing or finding a bass or bluegill under the shadows of a dock waiting for my juicy worm. Fishing … but I wasn't going fishing today, that's what I had told Bill Kelly that morning. Who was I kidding? I was born to fish. Fishing was all I could think about from the moment I got up on a summer's day until my eyes closed at night. Nothing could stop me. All I wanted to do now was get back to the lake.

When we got there, I had just enough time to walk down to my favorite dock. I threw a line out and watched the sun fall on the lake as if it was actually dropping into the far side. It was a peaceful and beautiful day on Rush Lake.

SɪX

Where did my childhood go so fast? It seems like just yesterday we were children playing games. I remember Mike and I were playing in Little League for the Yankees and Amy was dressing dolls. Now that my life is slowing down I have time to reflect and wish those days were still with me. When I pass a playground and watch the children, I think of the games we played as kids. Besides the normal hide and seek or neighborhood baseball or football games in the field next to our house, we made up some of our own.

One game was called Gobble-Gobble. It consisted of me, dressed mostly in black, running in the dark around the outside of the house chasing my brothers and sisters and most of the neighborhood kids as I made a loud strange scary noise with my throat. *"Gobble, gobble, gobble,"* I yelled as I chased them in the dark. If I caught one of them, I tackled them and tickled them on the ground until they laughed and screamed that they had enough. Another night game was to stand in Grandma Klein's front yard, look up into the night sky next to the huge Norway pine, and spin around until we were dizzy. When we stopped spinning, the whole world seemed to be spinning out of control and we would eventually fall to the ground. Lying on the ground and looking up into the night sky, it looked as if the massive tree was falling down on us.

The neighborhood baseball or football games were played down the street, usually with Bob and Spencer Kent. They were our best friends. We did a lot with Bob and Spencer. Even church. Not really our cup of tea, but they would invite us to so we could be part of the Royal Rangers and go on the camping trips or canoe trips that the elders of the church provided. The Cleavers, who lived close by, also joined in most games. The Cleavers had four boys that were all close in age. Mike, Stan, and Greg usually played with us, and Ron, the oldest, sometimes joined a team. We didn't like it when he did because he was older and bigger so he usually hit the ball deep over the road. With a few others that randomly showed up, we always seemed to have enough for two teams so we could play marathon games on summer or fall days. I'm sure we all remember them to this day.

Winters were hard. Cold blustery days and lots of snow made it almost impossible for anyone to make a living working outdoors. Grandma and Grandpa would close the resort after Thanksgiving and move to town. They wouldn't go back to the lake until late April to prepare the cabins for the Memorial Day opening. Dad worked the few jobs he could find indoors or finished jobs he had started in the fall. We didn't seem to want for anything. All or most of the groceries came from Peterson's General Store, where Dane Peterson was always kind enough to let us run a credit for anything he sold. Grandma and Grandpa Klein also helped by allowing us to share some of the whole frozen beef they bought each fall. We got by, and like the rest of nature in the north, we waited patiently for the thawing spring.

I remember when I was about nine, my dad decided to take the family to California for a few months during the winter so he could continue to build and earn money instead of going in debt while he waited for spring. With the help of our friends the Summers, Dad had a job waiting when we arrived. We packed up the brown Chevy station wagon and one morning in early January 1964, we started off cross-country. We left in the morning, and the thermometer hit twenty-seven below zero that night. We couldn't wait to leave for warm California.

We hit Route 66 somewhere outside of Chicago and never looked back. The days were long, hot, and boring, while the nights were strange cities full of flashing neon lights. The big anticipation each day was where we were going eat dinner and which motel we were going to stay in.

Motels with large bright signs of giant cowboys with lassos or restaurants with catchy names and flickering neon lights of cows or chickens were everywhere. Us kids usually helped picked the restaurant and motel but only after Mom and Dad agreed to the price. While the trip was long, we made it fun by hitting all the tourist traps and natural sights along the way.

When we made it to California, we found a house to rent at the end of a court. The backyard backed up to the school's playground, which made it a huge field. We quickly enrolled in school. That first day of school was the most embarrassing day of my life. Being rather shy, I was introduced to a class of full of strangers and heard giggling and whispering all around me. I think my face was red all day.

Klein family in Mexico

Soon, though, I fit in and made some friends. Mike and Amy did also. Our time in Pomona was great fun. Dad worked real hard all week He would come home exhausted and sometimes he sat in the kitchen in the evening after supper screaming with pain while my mom placed warm wraps on his painfully cramping muscles.

When the weekend came we always did something fun as a family. Disneyland, Knott's Berry Farm, the desert, and even Mexico were some of the fun places we would go. These were great times, meeting new friends, playing different kinds of games than back home, and, best of all, warm days in February.

I always remember that time as fun, but I also understand it was tough on my parents to attempt it at all. I couldn't imagine doing that myself. Funny, I guess the lack of money makes you attempt things in life that you wouldn't normally do, but after we did them, we were grateful they happened.

We headed for home in early May. The trip home was long and everyone was so homesick that we had lost all the excitement of the initial trip. The lights didn't look quite as bright, the days seemed a little longer. Each one just reminded us how far we were from home. We finally arrived back in Atlanta one late evening. The warm days of Pomona were distant memories and the wonderful spring of Michigan made us feel at home. We were all glad to be home. No Disneyland or Knott's Berry Farm, but home with friends and family and in our own beds.

Why do we wish for these past days of wonderment and youth? Is it because of their innocence and our feelings that life would last forever? The older people get, the more they appreciate their youth and all that it brought. In fact, late in life they sometimes try to resume some of their childhood by playing the games of earlier days.

I've often thought that childhood is the only time in our lives that we live day to day. Most of our lives are spent dreaming of the future and where it will take us. Ironically, when we get to the future, we dream of where we have been.

We look more to find family as we get older, family not only of blood, but family that have become blood. These people come in and out of our lives as if through revolving doors, and when they leave, they always seem to return to help us, unlike the passersby that may touch us for a moment now and then, only to leave and never be seen or heard of again. It is up to us to have the wisdom to accept these people that can become as an uncle or a brother. These people become part of the family over time. We have some of these people in our family. Joe and Mary have become a part of the family. Eric Wines has also earned a part in our family. He was Matt's best friend and took over the guitar playing at family reunions when Joe passed on. He and his new family have never missed a reunion since. Maybe all you really need to become part of our family is to be a guitar player!

The road home was getting too long and too emotional. I couldn't stop thinking of all the visitors I had seen today, people I hadn't thought about for years and others who seemed always to be in my thoughts. All of them seemed to be trying to tell me something without spelling it out. They gave me a sense that life after death did exist and that it wasn't a bad place. Funny thing, though, now that I think back on all the conversations I had today, not one of them mentioned God. Why? What did this mean? Then again, did I believe any of this today, or was I just in deep thought while driving home on such a beautiful day?

Religion was something that I always had trouble with. I always seem to use my scientific thinking, as I called it, to rationalize the truth of the Bible, the existence of the hereafter, or even the reality of God. I always had trouble believing in something that could only be explained by relying on faith. I needed a factual explanation to persuade me, not a belief.

My family follows many different dogmas. Some of their beliefs are laid out by a church, while others have been passed on as assumed moral doctrines of mothers and fathers from the past. Most of my family fall into the later category. Moral people, but not churchgoers. Some are not even church believers. Others are guided in their lives by a faith that helps them make sense of life with all its wonder and tragedy. No one argues either side. No one pushes their beliefs on another. We all accept the beliefs and ideas that each of us use as our personal moral guides.

OK … enough of all this religious stuff. I've got to get my mind on something else. I started thinking of Dad and the times I worked for him in the summers breaks from school. He had two speeds when he worked—fast and "Look out, Vern is on the job!" I never felt like we could keep up with him. Mike and I tried hard to impress him, but our efforts usually faded by mid-June when the heat and summer laziness hit our young minds and bodies. By August we were just waiting for school to start again. Anything but this! Dad had two sayings he used on us all the time: "Either do it or get out of the way and let someone else do it," or—my favorite—"Do something even if you do it wrong." He never took a day off because of illness. We always cherished the times he had to make a run for material or to visit a possible customer because he would be gone for some time and we could take a break, or at least take it easy. Days when we needed to pour concrete and it rained were even better. We got to sleep in and schedule nothing for the whole day!

"Greg, how have you been?" a voice suddenly came from the silence.

This time I was totally caught off guard by the source. It was Uncle Harvey, my dad's older brother. He was a big, fun guy when I was little, but he had a very addictive personality. The addictions slowly destroyed his life and his health. Alcohol was his burden to carry, but I always thought his real problem was his addiction to life. He was bigger than life, with a zest for telling stories in a loud booming voice and having fun anytime he and a few of his best friends got together. He was a handsome man with a business mind that, when focused on the task at hand, could make anything work.

"I'm fine," I said. "At least I think I'm fine." I was unsure after all that had happened today. "Long time since I've seen you." I answered as if I was uncomfortable and lost for words … which I was.

"Please don't remember me during all those bad times," he said. "That was not me. I was consumed by the urge of alcohol. It was something that destroyed me yet I didn't care at the time."

He went on, "I was the fun guy in your dad's backyard, making you a big three-inch thick rare burger on the grill and letting you have a drink of my beer to wash it down—even though you were ten at the time." He laughed at the memory. "Do you remember?" he said.

I did remember those times in the backyard at our house in town. He was fun, even though I never really got to know him very well. I also remember other times like Christmases at Grandma's or Uncle Merle's where he seemed to get louder the more he drank. He had a couple of failed business ventures in our town, and after a few tough years he divorced my aunt Evelyn and moved to the big city to try running a bar. Not a good idea for someone with a drinking problem. He met a new woman and tried to turn his life around. It soon fell apart and she left him as the addiction took control again.

The booze soon took over and he started his slow descent toward death until his final days, which were spent at a home somewhere outside of Atlanta, Georgia, where he quickly became a small shadow of himself. In the end he couldn't even recognize his own family. His death was quiet and not honored. No one was real proud of him at that low point of his life, but everyone understood this was not the man they grew up with and had grown to love.

"I watched out for your dad like a big brother when he was little," he told me. "I didn't have to watch him that close mainly because Betty was watching both of us. She was the big sister that anyone would be proud to have. She is watching out for me again and I am watching your dad."

Dad and Harvey

I told him I knew both my dad and Uncle Merle were proud of him and missed him. He listened intently to my words as if he was hoping they were true. He left the car quietly as if he was still embarrassed of his life. I understood and wished I could have known him better just to talk to him and to reassure him how his family and friends felt about him, but I didn't have the courage to do it. He was too much of a stranger, even though he was family. Funny, the roots were there but they weren't big enough or strong enough for me to feel comfortable talking to him. Life hadn't been fair to him. I try to always remember someone's life in the whole, remembering them mostly when they are shining in the glow of the sun and not in the cold and dark depths of their own hell.

I will always remember Uncle Harvey for his hearty laugh and his three-inch thick burgers.

Grandma and Grandpa Mowery with Roselyn, Glenn, and Mom

Mom and Dad's Wedding

Joe Cauchon and Aunt Betty

Grandpa Klein and Uncle Merle

Aunt Betty, Grandpa Mowery, and Uncle John

June and Betty Mowery, Mom and Great-grandpa Mowery

Mom and Aunt Rose

Seven

The brightly colored summers quickly faded. Grandma died suddenly after a short fight with cancer and Aunt Rose soon took ill and followed, succumbing to the weak heart that had plagued her frail body all her life. Uncle Glenn, reeling from the loss of his only son little Glenn to a fatal car wreck just days after Little Glenn's wedding, moved to Florida and along with the rest of his family, lived in seclusion with the pain of what might have been.

Grandpa Mowery sold his resort in small pieces and moved into a trailer that he placed on top of the hill overlooking Little Lake. His mind played tricks on him from time to time throughout his life, but after the deaths of his wife and daughter, a dam broke inside his head. He turned into a different person, not like family anymore. He acted like he didn't like us, and even though we realized it was his mind and not his true self, it was hard for us. We lost touch with him during that terrible time. He was conned by a much younger gold-digger and spent a lot of his money on her and her kids. He was finally admitted to a mental institution after she left him and his condition worsened. He had to spend a lot of time there. My mom was relieved to have him finally in custody, even though she knew it would be a long time before he was well again.

We also lost touch with Clifford. He didn't come up to the lake as often. He seldom came to stay at the cabin he had built for Rose just a few years before her death. He looked for someone that could take her place, but sadly, no one even came close. Some even took advantage of the quiet kindness that Aunt Rose had admired in him during their short time together.

Our family had grown up and the older kids began to focus on other priorities, like sports and school activities, and of course, the opposite sex. The two youngest kids in our family, Rick and Matt, came along too late to enjoy the wonderful summer days of Rush Lake, missing the times that had become embedded in our memories and dreams. Grandpa's mind recovered for the final time late in his life. It was in that short period of time before his death that Rick and Matt established a relationship with him, but the rest of us knew he was nothing like the man we remembered. He was an old man living mostly in the quiet past and in a world none of us understood.

In his last few years, he lived like a child in a home for the elderly, making simple crafts and worrying about his access to his cigarettes, which the nurses were trying to hide from him as much as possible. I never understood why they would not give someone late in their life something which they desired. The few times he came to our house to spend a few hours with the family, he could barely hold a conversation or stay long enough without tiring from the exhaustion of breathing.

Looking back on this time of departure, I think Aunt Rose was the key. She held all the characters together like glue with her charm and personality, and when she was gone, we fled the lake, each in our own way. People like her come along once in a lifetime and with their passage, the invisible force that ties people together is reduced. Everyone flies out into outer orbits as if they are planets hurtling into lonely space. I think Grandma was right in the observation earlier today that we are all tied together through a brighter side. I am starting to understand how important it is for all of us to honor these invisible ties. The roots that tie us all together can disappear as time moves on. What makes them disappear? Why can't they keep each of us close any longer? In this case, the pain of memories pushed us from the lake and dissolved the roots. The pain of people leaving when we didn't want them to leave will do strange things to people. My mom can attest to that.

I remember a scene from the movie *Harvey* where Elwood P. Dowd told the rabbit, "Mother always told me you must be oh-so-smart or oh-so-pleasant. Well, for years I was very smart. Harvey, I recommend pleasant."

Pleasant was Roses' way. Aunt Rose once told me never to talk bad about anyone unless they were on a daytime soap. That way you would never hurt anyone's feelings, and most of those soap opera people deserved it. She loved her soaps and whenever any of her friends in the trailer park stopped by, they would chat about the latest developments in wild detail as if they knew the characters personally.

Rose had few friends while she lived in Detroit, so the times she spent up north with family were always special. Holidays and a couple of weeks during the summer were the best they could do because of Clifford's demanding job. Christmases were the best. Any time she had a stage to display her practical jokes, she would not miss the opportunity. A typical trick was to give a large, wrapped gift that turned out to be full of nothing but newspaper. She would also cut very, very small pieces of pie, set them in front of us kids, and act like nothing was wrong, or completely skip someone at the table when serving dessert. One cold Christmas day she asked Grandma to come outside to see something. Grandma cautiously followed, and when she stepped off the porch, Rose ran back in, shut the door, and locked her out in the cold. Grandma was what P.T. Barnum said was born every minute: a sucker. Could it be she was like the rest of us, a bit player on Roses' stage of life? We all played into her hands. She demanded that life go her way, funny and exciting with no pauses, as if she knew it was going to be short and we humored her because we all wanted to be part of it for as long as it lasted.

It didn't last long enough. When she died, the void she left seemed to force people to move in different directions, mostly away—not because they wanted to, but because they had lost the deep feeling of family and friends that made them want to stay. The warmth she used was mixed with humor and love. Rush Lake would never be the same. I was never the same …

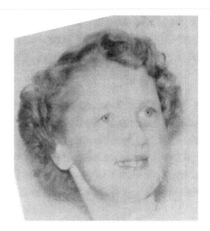

Aunt Rose—now might I see you?
Will your withered body come anew?
Touching thrice the things you pass,
as if to remember a familiar mood.
Heaven grew silent when you died,
making lives seem painfully sane.
In the night the lonely loon cried;
time stopped except for the rain.

Aunt Rose—now might I see you?
Ghosts of my family gathered today.
We came to toast your momentary life,
and to raise a glass of champagne.
We gathered dressed in suits of black—
you attract us like moths to a flame.
Time will keep you forever inside,
Aunt Rose—I hope to see you again.

"Poor Harvey!" a voice came out of the dream. Aunt Betty appeared. She was my dad's older sister.

"Why poor Harvey?" I asked.

"He was a poor lost soul," she said. "He's now himself again, A good man and a good brother, but it's too late to prove this to all he left on earth."

He did seem different, I thought. He seemed to be like the guy who used to make people laugh and laugh with a hearty roar. Maybe she was right. "I wished I had known him better, Aunt Betty."

"He was a good man inside, Greg. I lived with two people who had addictions that ruined their lives and those around them. They were good people, just not when the drink drove them to their bad side."

"Who was the other one?"

"My first husband, Clair. He was a good man but drinking made him unbearable. Same with Harvey."

"You had an addiction, didn't you Aunt Betty?"

"Yes, how good of you to remember, Greg," she said, laughing. "Cigarettes made my later years hell. You remember the oxygen bottle? It is not the way you want live, tied to a tube. I'm better now … just like Harvey."

"It's good seeing you, Aunt Betty," I said changing the subject.

She had been a teacher just like her mother. She was always a very pretty woman, very classy. When I was a little boy, I always thought she was a model. She had lived two lives. The first one was with Clair, an alcoholic, and she had raised three boys. The other life was with Uncle Johnny, who I had known better. He was a lawyer and a scholarly type who worked for NASA. His stories were very exciting to hear because he was a big part of the moon launch. He was quiet and had a dry sense of humor. Betty and Johnny didn't fit together, yet they happily lived hand-in-glove for the rest of their lives.

"Good seeing you too, Greg," she said. "Looks like you have had a busy day, haven't you?"

"How did you know?"

"Questions, questions, questions, in due time …"

I wanted to talk to her for a bit before she left so I didn't pause too long to let her get away. "Every time I see the house behind Mom and Dads at the lake I think of you and Uncle Johnny," I said.

"You know, Greg," she said, "those were some the happiest years of my life. Traveling between Zephyrhills and Lake Fifteen gave us a lot of wonderful times with friends and family. Your Uncle Johnny opened up a lot living around your family. He and his dog Snook loved to visit your family most mornings. He really liked Matt and that crazy dog Curley. I was also a lot closer to my family for the first time in a long time. My boys came to visit many times and Merle and Vernon were right next door. They were great times while they lasted." She added, "Do just one thing for me, Greg—please don't remember people in a bad way. Try to always see the good in people."

She started to talk again about living with people you can't help. "Greg, another piece of advice … live for yourself and the ones who love you. Don't waste your time with people who don't care for themselves."

Uncle Johnny and Aunt Betty

I didn't question it. I had to believe her, even though she hadn't done it in her life. She spent much of her life worrying about others.

"I love my boys, Eddie, Butch and Bob. Butch and Bob created wonderful lives for themselves but Eddie needed help and I couldn't help him." She paused and reflected about something from long ago and deep inside, then replied in a tone that sounded like failure on her part. "No one could, you see. No one can help people who can't help themselves. Someday soon I won't need to help Eddie anymore."

I watched as she poured her heart out and as she talked I suddenly saw a glimpse of her mother's face. She said she had to go and help someone. With that, she left.

I don't know why she talked so much about all the people in her life that she hadn't been able to help. I guess she had to deal with a lot of people that needed help and she felt like a failure. She wasn't. She was warm and caring.

Once again someone had left without saying good-bye or answering any of my questions. I even forgot to ask how Uncle Johnny was doing. Who did she have to help? I hadn't seen her for so long, and I had too many questions and too many feelings to have her leave so quickly. My urge to talk to her about everything was left unsatisfied. But why should it be any different? This was the way it had happened to me all day. I knew a bottle of wine was on tap for me tonight when I got home, and I muttered, "I'm going to need it!"

I peered ahead to see the small road sign in the distance. Gradually the writing came into focus. I was stunned.

Lansing, sixty-nine miles.

Eight

"Did you think I wouldn't come to see you?" The voice was vaguely familiar but teasingly distant so that I had to turn to confirm my suspicions. There she was. Tiny, frail, and delicate looking but with big rosy cheeks and glasses that didn't quite fit her face. A big smile that made me feel warm inside like everything in the world was suddenly peaceful. I studied her face to see if I could remember all the nuances that triggered memories during restful naps. It had been a long time since I had seen her and I just wanted to drink in some of the moment.

"I knew after all the people I've had in this car today I would be seeing you soon," I said. "I don't know where to start. How have you been?" How have you been? How stupid was that? I started the conversation like I was talking to an old friend from school whom I didn't have much in common with anymore.

"Wonderful," she replied. "Relax, this place is a great place to be. You feel great all the time and you get to see anyone you want anytime. And helping people throughout their lives is very rewarding."

"Place? What place? What are you talking about?" I asked.

"Greg, I was sent here to tell you what is happening and why all those people have suddenly been coming to you today," she said.

"Do you mean there's a reason for all these strange meetings today? What?" I asked. But somehow I didn't really want to hear her answer. I just wanted to sit and talk about old times and laugh like I had done with her so many times before.

"Do you remember the deer on the road this morning?" she asked.

"Yes, a few hours ago. It sure was a close call." I answered, reliving the feeling I had had when it happened.

"Too close," she said, continuing with the truth that I didn't want to hear. She told me that I had swerved to miss the deer and hit a big oak tree square on. She went on to explain that I had died instantly. Numbly, I listened to her words as she explained how you are slowly brought to the realization that you have died. It was one of the wonderful ways this place works. Too much, too fast, and you might not accept it. She continued talking with all the excitement of a youngster explaining how she got lost in a candy store. On the other hand, I was having trouble keeping my thoughts from wandering to other people. How would they get along without me? How would they survive? Debbie? My kids? My dogs? Who would take care of them?

"Don't worry about anyone else," Aunt Rose said, as if reading my mind. "They will all be fine. They will be helped though life."

"They will be helped though life?" I asked. "By whom?"

She continued with the explanation and I found myself becoming more and more interested in her illustration of the place I am now part of. People who die are assigned to watch and protect others in their circle of family and friends. Sometimes they are assigned three or four people to watch, depending on their family size or friends they left behind. She explained how the Bible is somewhat correct in that god is everywhere and with you at all times. I asked if the god she was referring to was really the God everyone read about from the Bible. "Not quite," she said. She explained that all religions were good for humanity in their own way, but there wasn't a single entity. We think God, Buddha, or Allah is watching over us, as if they are humanlike, but the real god is within all of us all the time. All of our souls combine into a large powerful force we call it the *Soul*, pronounced the same in whatever language you speak. We are all connected, but when we die we become truly connected. "I think you were told that by Grandma earlier today," Aunt Rose continued. "You were born with your own god inside. This information becomes instinctual to you once you die. Your beliefs and your morals were part of the makeup of your god on earth, but faith is the key to all religions. Without faith, mankind would be destroyed. When you die and become part of the Soul, you're assigned to someone. This assignment is made by all those that knew you either by family ties or as close friends. Roots … these are the roots everyone was referring to. If you have no family or friends, you are passed on to the next level automatically."

"Is this why we say the soul never dies?" I asked.

"Not really," she said. "That is an earthly idea, but I think people on earth wish it to be the truth."

"Were you assigned to me?"

"No, you were David's assignment," she said.

"David … David my brother?"

"Yes," she replied.

"Where is he?" I asked.

"He is now moving on to the next level. Most children are automatically assigned to the next person in their family that will come here," she explained.

"You know that information, who's going to die next?"

"We know everything we need to help people."

"Why didn't he save me? Why did I die?"

"You can't stop someone from dying, but you can help them through the lonely and desperate times." She explained that the departed live their lives through the person they care for. "He lived with you and within you, throughout all the good and bad times, and this way he continued on earth."

My head was swimming with questions. The numbing was subsiding and being replaced with confusion.

"So the Bible is not true?" I asked.

"Not entirely ... but parts of it." She went on to explain that all religious writings are encounters by people telling stories that grew fictionally throughout the years. The basic concepts are true. There is an all-encompassing force watching over all of us. We do go to a wonderful place. The Soul is in all of us and combines to create the almighty god.

"Do you watch just anyone?"

"No, you are assigned a family member or a friend unless you don't have anyone left."

"So do all children help?" I asked.

"Not always. They can be sent right through. It depends on our decision. Same as animals. If they had special importance to you, they will be there when you arrive. All the others are passed through. Bad people are always passed through, never to become a part of the Soul."

She added, "Their lives will never become substantial and we never want them watching or helping. They move to a different level of their own. It's not a bad place, not like we think of hell, but they will never come in contact with others, forever banished."

I realized that I hadn't felt that I was now a part of the Soul that Aunt Rose was describing. I didn't feel any different than I had this morning. She explained why. I hadn't been *touched* by the Soul yet. This usually happens after the newly departed person is completely accepting of his or her fate. "After a short time to accept it, you will be *touched* and feel as if everything everywhere is happening inside you and all the ties to mankind will be plugged in," she said, adding, "It will be the most wonderful feeling you could imagine. You will then start watching someone that was assigned to you by the Soul until they die and come to join us."

"Do you see everyone here, like Abe Lincoln or Albert Einstein?" I asked.

"No, just your family and friends from life."

"What is the next level you keep mentioning?"

"It is a wonderful place that remains like the days you lived on earth, only forever. It is considered truly like Heaven."

I didn't question the explanation. I accepted everything she said. I wanted to ask her about everything. I wanted answers. I also enjoyed seeing her and being there with her so close. I wanted to reach out and hug her.

"Don't hug me yet, not until you are ready."

She was listening to my thoughts. She was right, I wasn't ready. That would have made me part of the Soul. There were still too many questions running through my mind. Most importantly, I suddenly came to the realization that I was not alive anymore! This really hadn't set in yet. I had left the earth. I was gone. What about my family? Debbie was all alone! Who would take care of my kids, how would everyone get along without me? Panic struck me and I didn't know what to do about the sick feeling deep inside. A song was playing in my head, a lyric from Bobby Darin, one of Mom's favorite singers. Where was this music coming from? The words were haunting because they were from his last song of his last performance.

Off comes the makeup
Off comes the clown's disguise
The curtains falling
The music slowly dies
But I hope you're smiling
As you're filing out the door …

I think we're all smiling as we file out the door. People like Aunt Rose and Joe Couchon leave us that way. They add spice to life. I then realize the music is coming from the radio in my car and I'm driving down the road again. I peer ahead to see a little boy walking toward me in the middle of the road. He was walking straight at me as if he was not afraid. I stopped the car in front of him and stepped out quickly to question who he was. His face looked very familiar but I had never met him before. He smiled and spoke to me when he got close enough.

"You don't know me, do you, Greg?" he said, as if he knew me.

"I don't think so, should I?" I asked.

"Yes, my name is David."

With those words, my heart sank deep inside my chest. I couldn't believe it. Here is someone I had never met but he had spent a lifetime watching out for me and my family. Studying his face, I could see the rest of my family in every corner. He had my mom's eyes. He was a beautiful child. Why wasn't he older? He should be older than me.

"It's good to meet you and thanks so much for watching over me." That was the only thing I could think to say to him.

"I didn't just watch out for you, I lived within you. I lived my life through you and enjoyed everybody and everything … so thank you, thank you so much," he said. "You're not afraid to be here are you?" he asked as if he saw my anxiety. "Don't be," he answered before I could reply. His answer was simple but somehow very reassuring. Talking with him made me feel as comfortable and warm as if I were lying in the sun on a dock at Rush Lake.

"You won't miss anyone anymore and the best is yet to come."

How could the best be yet to come when I had just found out that I had crashed my car and died? I'm not sure yet, but I don't think that is a good thing. All I wanted to do was get back in my car and finish the trip home to Indiana where my wife and dogs were waiting.

I thanked him again and told him I must go. He seemed to understand. With that, I jumped back in my car, which was in perfect shape, no dents. I thought, *This is a huge nightmare and when I wake up, I will have one big laugh. Soul* I thought ... though it did make sense. It did explain all the religious beliefs around the world and how they all tied into each other. *Let me start this car and get on my way home.* Turning the key, I heard Aunt Roses' voice again.

"This is why we let you accept it slowly." I turned to see her sitting next to me again as if she had never left. My head suddenly felt very heavy and tears began to flow down my face. I caught my heavy head with my hands and the emotions erupted. I started to cry uncontrollably. Aunt Rose told me not to worry, it happens to all of us. "Take some time and you will work it out."

I didn't want to be touched. I wasn't sure about this place.

I continued to cry with my head in my hands for what seemed like hours. When the crying subsided, I looked up to find Aunt Rose was gone. I was alone. *What do I do next? Who will come? Who will help me through this confusing dream?Dream? Is this all a dream? Will I wake up and find I am still driving home from this morning? Please God, let it be. God? Should I be praying to God ... or the Soul?* Driving down the road, I realized there weren't any other cars and the scenery didn't change. This wasn't a dream. *I am dead!* I need to work this out by myself and nobody can help me. Where is the acceptance going to come from?

I started to think of the days of Rush Lake again. Why is it that lake keeps pulling me back to its shores? Maybe that's where the answer lies. Maybe that's where the acceptance can be found. Maybe I need to let my mind wander to those summers long ago, where nights were cool and the grass was moist with dew. The air smelled sweet from the fragrance of today's flowers and from the trees and shrubs growing at a July's pace. It's there where the worries of a child were the hopes of his hero ballplayer hitting .300 or his favorite team making it to the World Series. His wonders were focused on the unknown aspects of the lake— the many unknown creatures that lived in and around the lake or the size of fish that might be caught but were still silently swimming in the dark depths of its waters. These are the thoughts that run through the mind of a young boy, a young boy whose life would be filled with many people with all types of personalities, but who loved each one in his or her own special way. Maybe that's the answer. Even though I am dead and in another place, I will be with all the people I knew in life, and here in this new place everybody is trying to get me to accept. The Soul makes that happen. It will keep me in touch with everybody that I care about and love. I will have the best of both worlds. The people still alive will be watched to make sure their days on earth are as wonderful as mine had been, and the thought that the others are in such a wonderful place made me feel happy. Why hadn't I seen this before? Why hadn't I put it all together? I realized the lake wasn't the answer, but it was a big part of the answer. The lake is a wonderful thing, but the people are what made the lake. That is why I never wanted to go back to revisit. The lake wasn't what I missed all those years. It was all those wonderful people, those loving, beautiful people. The lake was only there for all of us to find our way back to each other. The lake nurtured everything, including the roots that bind people together. That was why we were all drawn to the lake and felt so close to each other when we were there. It refreshed and strengthened our roots. I knew the answer now. I will miss Rush Lake forever, but for now I just wanted to be *touched* and start helping like the others here in this glorious place.

"You didn't take long," Aunt Rose said as she appeared next to me.

"No, I think it was because of the wonderful friends and family like I have. I'm not afraid of leaving anyone anymore. I see now … they have us to watch over them. I am ready now, I'm sure of it," I said as I turned toward the lady who had meant so much to me in my past and now would be with me forever in the future. Rose smiled and reached out hug me. As we embraced I felt the most amazing warmth start deep inside and suddenly flame into a light that became very bright around us. I was quickly consumed with so much knowledge that everything about life made sense. Love pushed all the hate, confusion, and pain out of my body. I felt totally connected to all of those who had known me in life, and now, also, with those here in this wonderful place.

Most of all, it felt good to be hugged by Aunt Rose again.

978-0-595-47346-5
0-595-47346-6

CPSIA information can be obtained at www.ICGtesting.com
Printed in the USA
LVOW08s0345230714

395533LV00002B/150/P